Margaret Ryan

Jemima
the Police Officer

Illustrated by
Caroline Crossland

PUFFIN BOOKS

PUFFIN BOOKS

Published by the Penguin Group
Penguin Books Ltd, 27 Wrights Lane, London W8 5TZ, England
Penguin Books USA Inc., 375 Hudson Street, New York, New York 10014, USA
Penguin Books Australia Ltd, Ringwood, Victoria, Australia
Penguin Books Canada Ltd, 10 Alcorn Avenue, Toronto, Ontario, Canada M4V 3B2
Penguin Books (NZ) Ltd, 182–190 Wairau Road, Auckland 10, New Zealand

Penguin Books Ltd, Registered Offices: Harmondsworth, Middlesex, England

First published 1993
1 3 5 7 9 10 8 6 4 2

Typeset by Datix International Limited, Bungay, Suffolk
Filmset in 16/19 pt Monophoto Palatino
Printed in England by Clays Ltd, St Ives plc

Contents

Jemima Sweet Goes to School

Jemima Sweet the police officer put on her smart black uniform and her smart black hat and set off for school. Today she was going to teach primary two all about road safety.

"I'm always very careful when crossing the road," one boy in the class told her. "I look both ways, and if it's all clear I walk smartly across."

"That's very good indeed," said Jemima.

"I'm always very careful when crossing the road," one girl in the class said. "I never cross near parked cars and I always look for the crossing."

"That's very good too," said Jemima. "Now take a partner and we'll all go outside and practise our road safety at the school crossing."

Primary two marched out in twos.

"What a pity you haven't got a partner," said another girl. 'Will you be all right on your own?"

"I think so,"smiled Jemima, and when it was all clear, she let primary two practise their road safety.

"Always look both ways before crossing," they reminded each other. And they did.

"Always wait for the green man," they chanted. And they did.

"Never dash out from behind lorries," they said. And they didn't.

"Well done," said Jemima. "You remember all these things and you're sure to be safe on the roads."

She was just about to take the children back into school when Susie Lee the district nurse arrived. She parked her Mini at one side of the road and ran across to the other.

"You didn't look both ways to see if it was safe to cross," all the girls said to her.

"You didn't wait for the green man," said all the boys.

"You're not safe on the roads," they all said together.

Susie Lee's face turned bright red. "Oh dear, you're quite right," she said. "I was

in such a hurry I didn't think."

"Don't worry, boys and girls," said
Jemima. "I'll show Susie Lee how to cross
the road properly."

And while the children chanted all the
safety rules, Jemima took Susie Lee's hand
and led her safely across the road. Then

Susie Lee promised not to forget what she'd learned, and, her face still pink, she hurried away.

"Well done, boys and girls," said Jemima.

She was just about to take them back into school when Mr Gupta came out of his takeaway and hurried across the road.

"You didn't look to see if it was safe to cross," all the girls said to him.

"You didn't wait for the green man," said all the boys.

"You're not safe on the roads," they all said together.

Mr Gupta's face turned bright red. "Oh goodness, you are quite right," he said. "I was in such a hurry I didn't think."

"Don't worry, children," said Jemima. "I'll show Mr Gupta how to cross the road properly."

And while the children chanted all the safety rules, Jemima took Mr Gupta's hand and led him safely across the road. Then Mr Gupta promised not to forget what he had learned, and, his face still pink, he hurried away.

"Well done, boys and girls, I'm really pleased with you," said Jemima, and she was just about to take the children back into school when along the road came a large lady in a bright green coat and hat, pushing a twin pushchair.

"Look, Jemima," said all the children. "Here comes your mum with Susie and Sam."

"Hullo, Susie and Sam. Hullo, Mum," said Jemima. "I was just teaching the children the rules of road safety and showing them the safe way to cross the road."

"And a good thing too," said her mum. "Maybe I'd better make sure that you know how to do it properly yourself, Jemima." And she took Jemima's hand and led her safely across the road.

Then Jemima's face was red, and all the children laughed and chanted, "Jemima's crossing safely with her green mum."

Jemima's Traffic Duty

Jemima Sweet the police officer pulled on her orange bib and her orange armbands and sighed.

"I don't like traffic duty at the crossroads," she said to her husband, William, as he pulled on his overalls for his job at Big Ed's garage. "All the cars and lorries and buses get into such a muddle and make such a noise."

"Perhaps the traffic won't be so bad today," said William. "Cheer up and give me a smile."

But Jemima didn't cheer up and she didn't give William a smile. She just sighed again, and set off for the crossroads.

The traffic at the crossroads was terrible. All the cars were tooting, all the lorries were hooting and all the buses were going HONK HONK HONK. Jemima shook her head, took a deep breath, and strode out into the middle of the road.

"You can come on," she signalled one line of traffic.

"Stay where you are," she ordered another.

"And just where do you think you're going?" she asked a little blue Mini which was trying to sneak past.

After a while she got the traffic flowing smoothly, and she cheered up, and gave a little smile.

But it didn't last.

At that moment Peter Potts the plumber arrived in his little red van and parked it on a single yellow line, right beside the sign that said NO PARKING.

"I know I shouldn't park there, Jemima," he said. "But I have to deliver this new bathroom suite to number twenty-one. I promise I won't be long."

"Oh, all right then," said Jemima as all the cars started tooting, all the lorries started hooting, and all the buses started going HONK HONK HONK as they

16

tried to squeeze past Peter Potts's little red van.

After a while Peter drove away. Then Jemima got the traffic flowing smoothly again, and she cheered up and gave a little smile.

But it didn't last.

At that moment Enoch Twyce the postman arrived in his big red post office van and parked it on a double yellow line, right beside the sign that said NO PARKING AT ANY TIME.

"I know I shouldn't park there, Jemima," he said, "but I have to deliver these new telephone directories to all the shops and houses. I promise I won't be long."

"Oh, all right then," said Jemima as all the cars started tooting, all the lorries started hooting, and all the buses started going HONK HONK HONK as they tried to squeeze past Enoch Twyce's big red van.

After a while Enoch drove away. Then Jemima got the traffic flowing smoothly again, and she cheered up and gave a little smile.

But it didn't last.

At that moment a great big red recovery van drove up and parked on a triple yellow line, right beside the sign that said, NO PARKING AT ANY TIME EVER. Then the driver jumped out and ran into one of the nearby shops.

"Well, of all the cheek," said Jemima as all the cars started tooting, all the lorries started hooting, and all the buses started going HONK HONK HONK, as they tried to squeeze past the great big red recovery van. "I'll take down that driver's name and number. He's certainly not delivering anything."

"Oh, yes, he is," said the driver, suddenly appearing at her side. "He's delivering these to you to cheer you up and make you smile."

And he handed Jemima a huge bunch of golden daffodils.

"Oh, William, it's you," said Jemima. "You are sweet."

And she cheered up right away, and gave her husband a great big smile.

This time it did last.

And all the people in the cars and lorries and buses stopped tooting and hooting and honking and shouted, "HAPPY TRAFFIC DUTY, JEMIMA."

Jemima's Crime Prevention Talk

It was a fine summer's evening and Jemima's twins Susie and Sam were having tea in the garden.

"Sit still and eat up, you two," said Jemima, pouring out their milk. "And stop stuffing mashed potato up your noses."

The twins grinned, and their dad, William Sweet, laughed. "You go inside and look over your talk for tonight, Jemima," he said. "I'll feed the twins."

"All right," said Jemima. "You know I'm really quite nervous about giving this talk, William. I hope I don't forget anything."

Two hours later, clutching her notes, Jemima got into her police car and drove to the town hall. Outside the town hall was a big notice. It said:

TONIGHT 7.30 p.m.
CRIME PREVENTION
A TALK
BY
W.P.C. JEMIMA SWEET

"Oh dear," said Jemima when she saw the big notice. "I really do hope I don't forget anything."

Just inside the town hall's big doors she met Mr Gupta from the takeaway.

"Good evening, Jemima," he said. "What a lot of notes you've got there. Are you going to tell us to use a security pen to

22

write our postcode on all our valuables, so
that we'll recognize them if they're
recovered after a robbery?"

Jemima looked at her notes. "Yes," she
said. "I was going to tell you that."

"Good," said Mr Gupta. "I'll look
forward to hearing it."

23

Jemima went on into the lecture room. Just inside the swing doors, she met old Mrs Hargreaves.

"Hullo, Jemima," said old Mrs Hargreaves. "What a lot of notes you've got there. Are you going to tell us old folks to get a peep-hole and a chain on our front doors and not to open them to strangers?"

Jemima looked at her notes. "Yes," she said. "I was going to tell you that."

"Good," said old Mrs Hargreaves. "I'll look forward to hearing it."

Then Jemima headed towards the platform. She was nearly there when out of a side door came Peter Potts the plumber.

"Hi there, Jemima," he said. "What a lot of notes you've got there. Are you going to tell us not to leave ladders and tools outside in our gardens in case thieves use them to break into our houses?"

Jemima looked at her notes. "Yes," she said. "I was going to tell you that."

"Good," said Peter Potts. "I'll look forward to hearing it."

Then Jemima stepped up on to the
platform. She cleared her throat, crossed
her fingers, and gave her Crime
Prevention talk. She didn't forget to tell
them all about marking their valuables
with their postcode, and Mr Gupta
beamed at her. She didn't forget to tell
them all about locking their doors and
staying safe, and old Mrs Hargreaves
beamed at her. She didn't forget to tell
them all about putting away their ladders

and tools to help prevent burglaries, and Peter Potts beamed at her. In fact she didn't forget anything at all, and the talk went very well. When it was over, Jemima gave a sigh of relief and gathered up her notes. She was just stepping down from the platform when old Mrs Hargreaves stood up.

"One moment, Jemima," she said. "Before you go, can I ask a question?"

"A question," said Jemima. "Oh dear, Mrs Hargreaves. Yes, of course. I'll answer it if I can."

"Do Susie and Sam still like to stuff mashed potato up their noses?"

Jemima Bakes a Cake

It was Jemima's day off, and she decided to bake a sponge cake.

"We'll help," said the twins, Susie and Sam, and they put on their big red helping aprons.

"I'll help," barked the old English sheepdog, Hairy Sweet, and stuck out his big pink tongue to help eat anything tasty that fell.

"We'll have the cake for tea," promised Jemima as she got out the margarine and eggs, sugar and flour.

Susie and Sam helped by pouring the sugar into the mixture and stirring it around. Hairy helped by licking up the fallen sugar.

Soon the mixture was ready and Jemima put it into the baking tin and popped it into the oven.

"Now we have to be patient and wait till the cake is ready," she said.

Before long, the delicious smell of baking sponge cake was floating all round the house.

It floated under the button noses of Susie and Sam as they played with their building bricks.

"Yum yum," they said. "We can't wait to taste that sponge cake, but we have to wait till it's ready."

The delicious smell floated under the big black nose of Hairy Sweet as he lay snoozing on the hearthrug.

"Yum yum," he barked. "I can't wait to taste that sponge cake, but I have to wait till it's ready."

The delicious smell even floated under the long nose of Jemima Sweet as she washed up the mixing bowl in the sink.

"MMMMMM," said Jemima. "I can't wait to taste that sponge cake. I wonder if it's ready yet? I'll just take a quick peek and see."

She opened the oven door and the sponge cake, which had been rising beautifully, collapsed with a SSSSSSSIGH back into its tin.

"Oh, no," said Jemima. "Just look at the sponge cake, it's as flat as a pancake. Now what shall we do with it?"

She thought for a moment, then she gave a little smile as she always did when she had a good idea.

"I know," she said. "We'll take it to the park and feed it to the ducks."

"Feed it to the ducks? What about feeding it to us?" said Susie and Sam and started quacking like ducks. QUACK QUACK QUACK.

"Feed it to the ducks? What about feeding it to me?" barked Hairy Sweet, and tried quacking like a duck. QUOOF QUOOF QUOOF.

But Jemima took no notice, and just popped the twins into their pushchair, popped Hairy on to his lead, and set off for the park.

The park was busy with people walking, busy with children talking, busy with ducks

squawking as they waddled after the
crumbs that were thrown to them.

"Oh dear," said Jemima, "these ducks
are getting very fat. Everyone seems to be
feeding them today."

She got out the flat sponge cake, and
was just going to call over the ducks
when behind her came the sound of
running feet. Then . . .

"PEEEEP PEEEEP," went a police
whistle.

"Stop, thief," yelled a police constable, as he chased after a man running away with a lady's handbag.

Jemima didn't hesitate. "Mind the twins, Hairy," she said, and as the thief ran past she stuck out a foot.

THUD, the thief hit the ground. THUMP, Jemima sat on top of him. SSSSSSSSS, the thief let out a SSSSSSSIGH like an ovenful of collapsing sponge cakes.

"Thanks, Jemima," said the police constable as he took over and led the thief away. "Lucky you were in the park today."

"Lucky my sponge cake didn't work out," laughed Jemima. "I was just going to feed it to the ducks. Now where did I put it? I'm sure I put it down, but I can't see it anywhere."

She looked down on the path but the cake wasn't there. She looked down on the grass, but the cake wasn't there either. She even looked down into her dress pockets, but the sponge cake had vanished.

"That's funny," said Jemima. "I wonder where it's gone?" She looked at Hairy and Susie and Sam. "Can any of you three see the sponge cake?"

Hairy and Susie and Sam all shook their heads. They couldn't see the sponge cake. Not now they'd eaten it. YUM YUM YUM.

Jemima Has Some Visitors

Jemima Sweet was on duty in the police station one afternoon, waiting for some very important visitors to arrive. Before long she heard them outside.

"I want to see the cells," said one small voice.

"I want my fingerprints taken," said another.

"I want to try on Jemima's police hat," said a third.

"And I want some good behaviour," said a teacher's voice, "or we'll turn right round now and go back to school."

Jemima smiled and opened the big glass doors to let the visitors in. She knew primary two from the local school, and their teacher, Mrs Mearns, very well.

"Hullo, Jemima," said the children. "We've come to visit you today. Can we see the cells? Can we have our fingerprints taken? Can we try on your hat?"

"One thing at a time," laughed Jemima. "I'll take you to see the cells first, but I don't think you'll want to stay there for very long."

They went down a big flight of stairs and down a long corridor.

"Here we are," said Jemima, and opened up the big heavy doors of the police cells to let the children see inside.

"There's no furniture," said one boy.

"There are no carpets," said one girl.

"And there's no sign of a telly," said the rest of the class.

"I'm afraid not," laughed Jemima. "Come on, follow me to the fingerprint room and have your fingerprints taken. That'll be more fun."

"This is much better," said the class, rolling up their sleeves and pressing their fingers into the black ink. "You can make some great fingerprints on this white paper. And it's really messy."

"Don't wipe your fingers on your

clothes," said Jemima and Mrs Mearns, but they were too late.

"Right," said Jemima when they'd all had a go. "Before you get to try on my hat, I want you to follow me again. I've got something rather special to show you."

Jemima led the way, down more long corridors, down more steep stairs, down into the back yard of the police station. The back yard was empty except for some small cages. The cages were empty except

for one. In it, all by himself, was a tiny
black and white puppy. He pawed at the
door of the cage and whined to get out,
and he nearly wagged his tiny tail off
when he saw the children.

"Oh, he's lovely," said the girls.

"Can we hold him?" said the boys.

"Does he have a name?" asked the teacher.

"I called him Benjy," said Jemima,
opening up the cage and handing the

puppy to the children to cuddle. "Hairy and I found him abandoned by the roadside this morning when we were out for our walk. He was miserable. Cold and wet and hungry. He hasn't been looked after at all."

"That's terrible," said the boys.

"That shouldn't be allowed," said the girls.

"That's right," said Jemima, "and unless I can find Benjy a good home where he'll be looked after properly I'll have to take him to the cat and dog home tonight."

"Don't worry, Jemima," said the children. "We'll tell our mums and dads all about Benjy when we go home from school. We'll find him a good home before tonight."

And Jemima didn't have to worry, because they did.

Jemima and the Loud Brass Band Music

It was a bright sunny morning, and Jemima Sweet the police Officer was just going on duty in the High Street when she spied Mr Gupta opening up his takeaway.

Jemima gave him a cheery wave. "Good morning, Mr Gupta," she called.

"Good morning? GOOD morning? I tell you, Jemima, it's not a good morning.

43

It's a very bad morning. But I'm really glad I met you. I've a complaint to make."

"Oh," said Jemima. "What's that?"

"It's old Mrs Hargreaves and her loud brass band music. All night long she plays it. BOOM TARARA BOOM TARARA BOOM TARARA BOOM. It can be heard half-way down the street. I can't get a wink of sleep, and without my sleep I'm a real grumpy-box."

"You can say that again," thought Jemima, but out loud she said, "I'll look into it, Mr Gupta."

Jemima turned her steps towards old Mrs Hargreaves's house, and met Enoch Twyce the postman out on his rounds.

Jemima gave him a cheery wave. "Good morning, Enoch," she called.

"Good morning? GOOD morning? I tell you, Jemima, it's not a good morning. It's a very bad morning. But I'm really glad I met you. I've a complaint to make."

"Oh," said Jemima. "What's that?"

"It's old Mrs Hargreaves and her loud
brass band music. All night long she
plays it. BOOM TARARA BOOM
TARARA BOOM TARARA BOOM.
It can be heard half-way down the street.
I can't get a wink of sleep, and without
my sleep I'm a real grumpy-box."

"You can say that again," thought
Jemima, but out loud she said, "I'll look
into it, Enoch."

Jemima hurried on to old Mrs
Hargreaves's house and half-way
down the street she heard the noise.
BOOM TARARA BOOM TARARA
BOOM TARARA BOOM. It sounded
like the brass band was marching up the
street. It wasn't, but the neighbours were.

"Oh, there you are, Jemima," they said.
"We're glad we met you, we have a
complaint to make."

"I know, I know," said Jemima. "I'll see what I can do."

She went up to old Mrs Hargreaves's front door and knocked very loudly. There was no reply. She went round to the back door and knocked louder still. Still there was no reply.

"She probably can't hear the knocking for the noise of the music," said Jemima to the neighbours.

Just then the back door opened and old Mrs Hargreaves let her cat, Charlie, out.

"Well," she said when she saw Jemima and the neighbours. "If you've all come for breakfast it'll just have to be tea and toast. I haven't got any cornflakes."

"We haven't come for breakfast, Mrs Hargreaves," said Jemima. "We've come about the noise from your brass band music."

"Oh, you've come to fix the music, Jemima. That's good. I think there must be something wrong with my cassette player, for no matter how much I turn up the sound I still can't hear the music. I can't get to sleep at night without the music playing, and without my sleep I'm a real grumpy-box. Do you think I should take the cassette player back to the shop and complain about it?"

"There's nothing wrong with the cassette player, Mrs Hargreaves," said Susie Lee the district nurse, appearing at Jemima's side. "It's your hearing aid that needs a new battery. Don't you remember I said I would bring you one?"

Susie Lee took the new battery from her nurse's bag and fitted it to the hearing aid.

Old Mrs Hargreaves put the hearing aid back on.

BOOM TARARA BOOM TARARA BOOM TARARA BOOM.

"Oh, my goodness," she said. "What's that terrible noise?"

"That's your music, Mrs Hargreaves," smiled Jemima. "It's a bit too loud. I think we'd better turn it down right away. We don't want the neighbours complaining."

Jemima's Night Duty

It was nearly eleven o'clock and Jemima Sweet the police officer was getting ready to go on night duty. She pulled on her waterproof jacket, put on her police officer's hat, and checked that her big torch was working.

"Night duty can be a bit boring," she said to her husband, William, as she climbed into her police car. "Sometimes there's nobody to talk to except on the radio, and nothing to do except check that everyone has remembered to lock up properly."

She waved to William and drove off. She had just stopped her police car and gone to see that Mr Gupta's takeaway was locked up properly, when Peter Potts the plumber drew up in his van.

"I'm on call for emergencies, Jemima,"
he said, "and Miss Wright's water tank
has burst and her kitchen ceiling's coming
down. Want to lend a hand?"

"Lead the way," said Jemima, and jumped
back into her police car and followed Peter
Potts to Miss Wright's house.

"Oh dear," said Jemima when she saw
the mess the water had made. "Come on,
Miss Wright, while Peter fixes your water
tank, I'll give you a hand to clear up."

When she had done that, Jemima climbed back into her police car and carried on with her patrol. She was just checking to see that the sports shop had been locked up properly when Susie Lee the district nurse drew up in her car.

"I'm on call for emergencies, Jemima," she said, "and Mrs Brown's new baby has decided to arrive in the middle of the night. Want to lend a hand?"

"Lead the way," said Jemima, and jumped back into her police car and followed Susie Lee to Mrs Brown's house.

"Oh, isn't she lovely," said Jemima when the baby was born and Susie Lee held her up for everyone to see. "Now I'll make us all a nice cup of tea."

When she had done that, Jemima climbed back into her police car and carried on with her patrol. She was just checking to see that the town hall had been locked up properly when she got a call on her radio.

"Proceed to McDonald's farm," said a crackly voice. "Possible intruder."

Farmer McDonald was out in his pyjamas and wellie boots when Jemima arrived.

"There's someone lurking round my big tractor making strange noises," he whispered. "Do you think they're trying to get it to start?"

"We'll soon find out," said Jemima, and got out her big torch.

Jemima and Farmer McDonald crept up to the big tractor. Sure enough, strange noises were coming from it.

"Do you think someone's trying to steal it?" whispered the farmer.

Jemima shone her big torch on to the tractor. "Not unless Daisybell can drive," she laughed, and patted the black and white cow who was munching some cheese sandwiches Farmer McDonald had left in the tractor at lunchtime.

Jemima helped Farmer McDonald lead Daisybell back to the barn, and checked that the barn door was locked up properly. When she had done that she climbed back into her police car and looked at her watch. It was nearly seven in the morning.

"Time I went home," she said. "That's my night duty over, and it wasn't a bit boring."

When she got home, she was just about to unlock her front door when the door swung open by itself.

"Oh no," said Jemima. "I should have started my night duty right here. William's forgotten to lock up our front door properly."

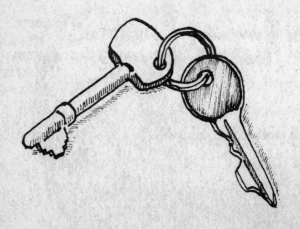

Jemima's Quiet Morning

It was a quiet Tuesday morning and
Jemima Sweet the police officer was on
early duty in the High Street. There was
hardly anyone about so Jemima stopped
to have a look in the toy shop window.

"I wonder what I should buy the twins
for their birthday," she said. "Those cuddly
teddies look nice, and so do those yellow
dumper trucks."

She was just admiring two toy police cars when old Mrs Hargreaves came trundling past with her shopping trolley.

"Morning, Jemima," she said. "Nice and peaceful this morning, isn't it?"

"Yes," said Jemima. "I like a morning like this."

Jemima walked on. All was still quiet so she stopped to look in the pet shop window.

"That reminds me," she said. "I must buy Hairy Sweet some more dog biscuits."

She was just looking at the price of the chocolate-covered ones when Enoch Twyce the postman came past with an empty sack.

"Morning, Jemima," said Enoch Twyce. "Nice and peaceful this morning, isn't it?"

"Yes," said Jemima. "I like a morning like this."

Jemima walked on. All was still quiet so she stopped to look in the sports shop window.

"William will need new football boots if

he's to play for the garage team," she said. "I
wonder if they've got a pair of big size tens."

She was just peering in the window to
see, when the peace of the morning was
shattered by a cackly voice calling . . .

"MORNING, JEMIMA. NICE
PEACEFUL MORNING, JEMIMA."

Jemima looked up. There, sitting on top
of a lamp-post, was Clarence, Peter
Potts the plumber's parrot.

"Oh, Clarence," said Jemima. "What are
you doing up there? You're not supposed
to fly about the High Street. Peter will be
looking everywhere for you. Come down
here to Jemima. Be a good boy."

But Clarence didn't want to be a good
boy. His beady eyes had spotted old Mrs
Hargreaves coming out of the baker's.
With a noisy sqawk, he swooped down
from the lamp-post, landed on her

shopping trolley and cackled . . .

"BOUGHT ANY BUNS? BOUGHT ANY BUNS?"

Old Mrs Hargreaves got such a fright, she dropped her shopping trolley, trod on her fresh cream doughnuts, and her flowery hat fell off and rolled into a puddle.

Clarence cackled with delight and flew back up on to the lamp-post.

Jemima sighed, picked up the trolley and the squashed doughnuts, then ran after the hat.

"Don't you worry, Mrs Hargreaves," she said, putting the hat back on the old lady's head. "You carry on with your shopping. I'll soon get Clarence." And she held out her right arm to the parrot and called, "Come down here to Jemima, Clarence. Be a good boy."

But Clarence didn't want to be a good boy. His beady eyes had spotted Enoch Twyce emptying the pillar-box. With a noisy squawk, he swooped down from the lamp-post, landed on the pillar-box and cackled . . .

"GOT ANY LETTERS? GOT ANY LETTERS?"

Enoch Twyce the postman got such a fright, he dropped his half-full sack, stood on some scattered letters, and his postman's hat fell off and rolled into the gutter.

Clarence cackled with delight and flew back up on to the lamp-post.

Jemima sighed, picked up the sack and the letters, then ran after the hat.

"Don't you worry, Enoch," she said, putting the hat back on the postman's head. "You carry on with your emptying. I'll soon get Clarence." And she held out her left arm to the parrot, and called, "Come down here to Jemima, Clarence. Be a good boy."

This time Clarence seemed to think about it, and with a noisy squawk he swooped down and landed, not on

Jemima's right arm, not on Jemima's left arm, but on her round police officer's hat, and he cackled . . .

"CAUGHT ANY BURGLARS? CAUGHT ANY BURGLARS?"

. . . which gave Jemima a fright, but she stood very still, and her hat didn't fall off because it was held on by elastic underneath her chin. Then she gave a little smile as she always did when she had a good idea, and she started walking very slowly down the High Street. Down to the end of the shops. Down to where Peter Potts the plumber lived.

Peter Potts was out in his garden searching for Clarence.

"Where are you, Clarence?" he was shouting. "You're making me late for work with this silly nonsense. Where are you?"

Jemima gave a little cough. "I think I may have what you're searching for, Peter," she said. "I found him in the High Street disturbing the peace."

Peter Potts looked up and saw Clarence sitting on Jemima's hat.

"Oh, I am sorry, Jemima," said Peter. "I'll see he doesn't fly off again. Now what do you say to Jemima for bringing you back home, Clarence?"

"SPOILSPORT," cackled Clarence.